Cats
Below the
Milky
Way

Published by MQ Publications Limited

12 The Ivories, 6–8 Northampton Street, London N1 2HY

Tel: 020 7359 2244 / Fax: 020 7359 1616

email: mail@mqpublications.com

ISBN: 1-84072-603-2

1 3 5 7 9 0 8 6 4 2

Printed and bound in Italy

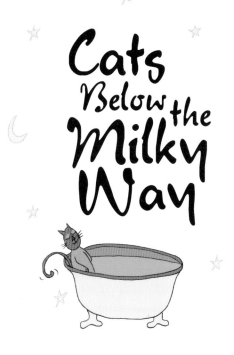

Cats
Below the
Milky
Way

BY LISA SWERLING & RALPH LAZAR

MQP

OLD FRIENDS.

I'll give him
ten for persistence,
ten for enthusiasm,
ten for resourcefulness,
but a straight zero for
understanding anything
about us!

THERE'S NO SUCH THING AS TOO MANY CATS.

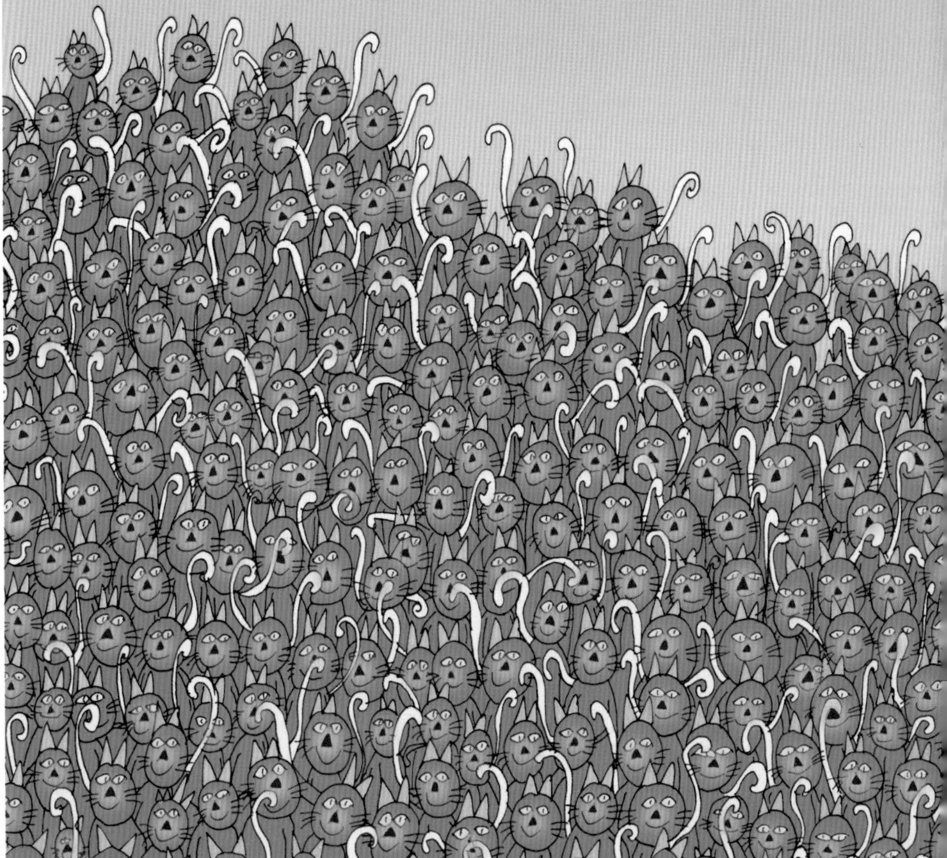

SYNERGY IN NATURE.

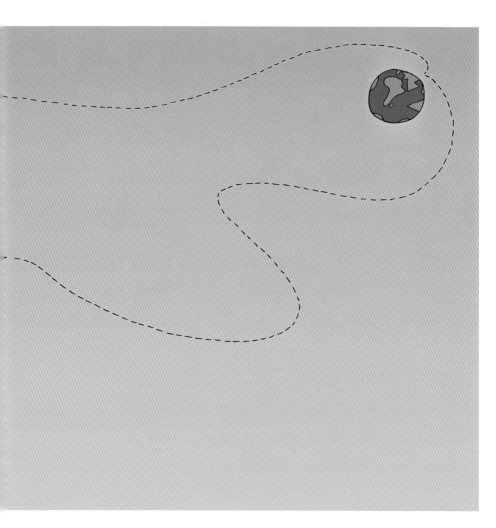

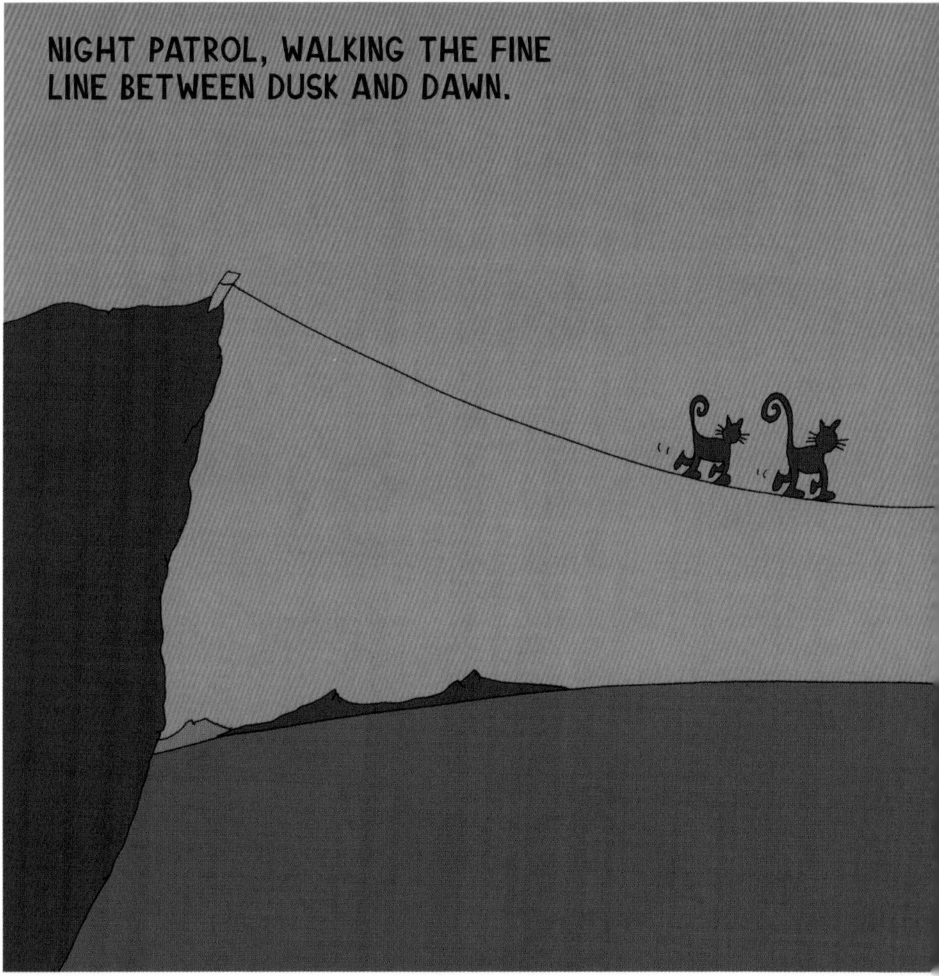
NIGHT PATROL, WALKING THE FINE
LINE BETWEEN DUSK AND DAWN.

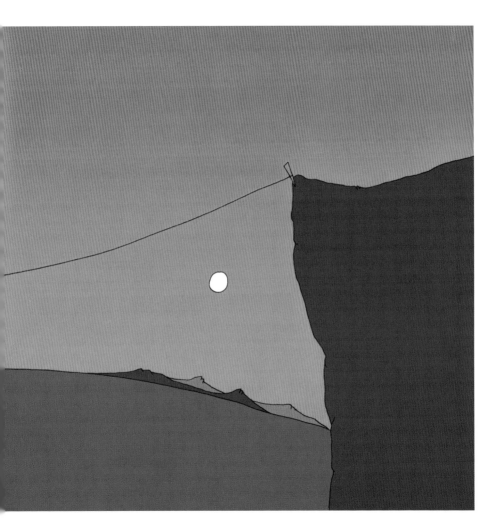

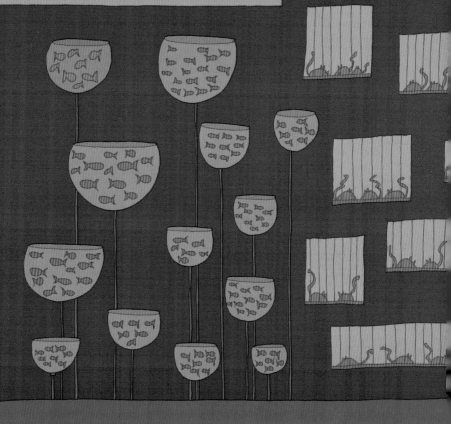

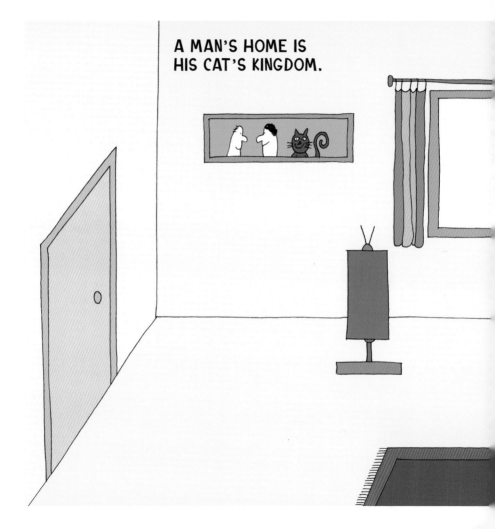

THE WORLD ACCORDING TO HUMANS.

THE WORLD ACCORDING TO CATS.

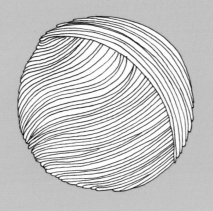

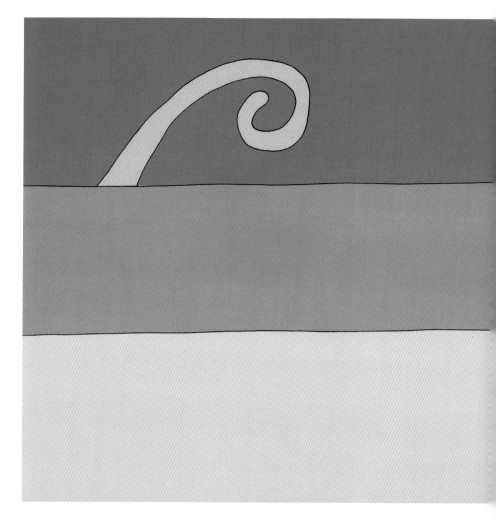

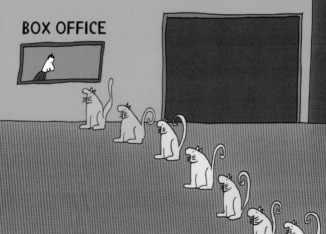

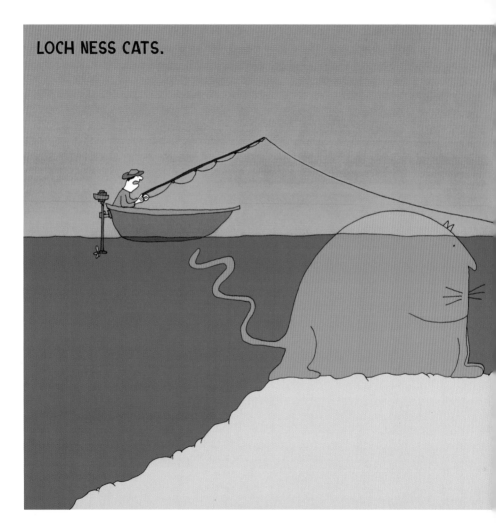

LOCH NESS CATS.

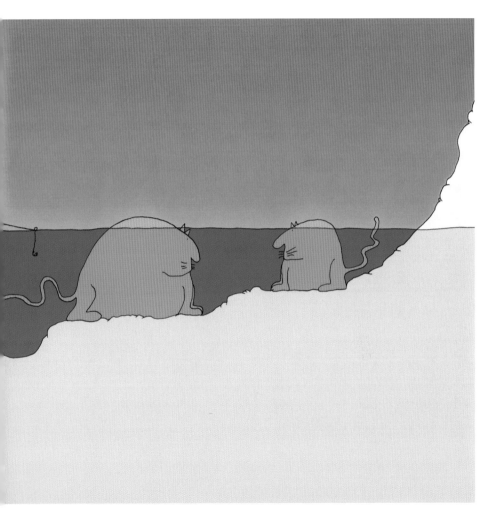

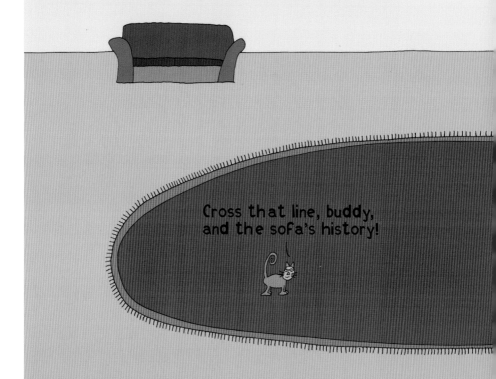

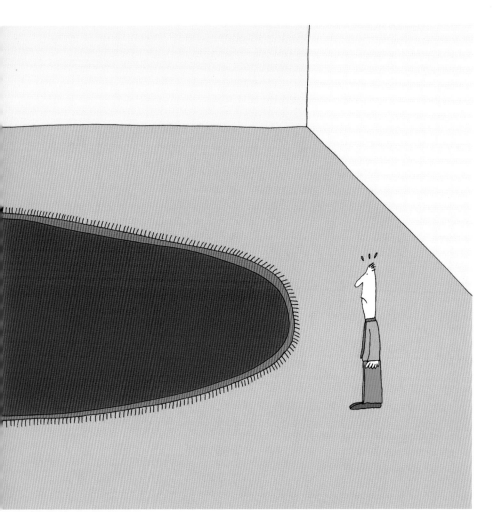

CAT WITH PhD (Perpetual head-scratching device).

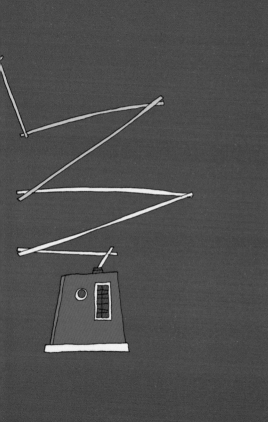

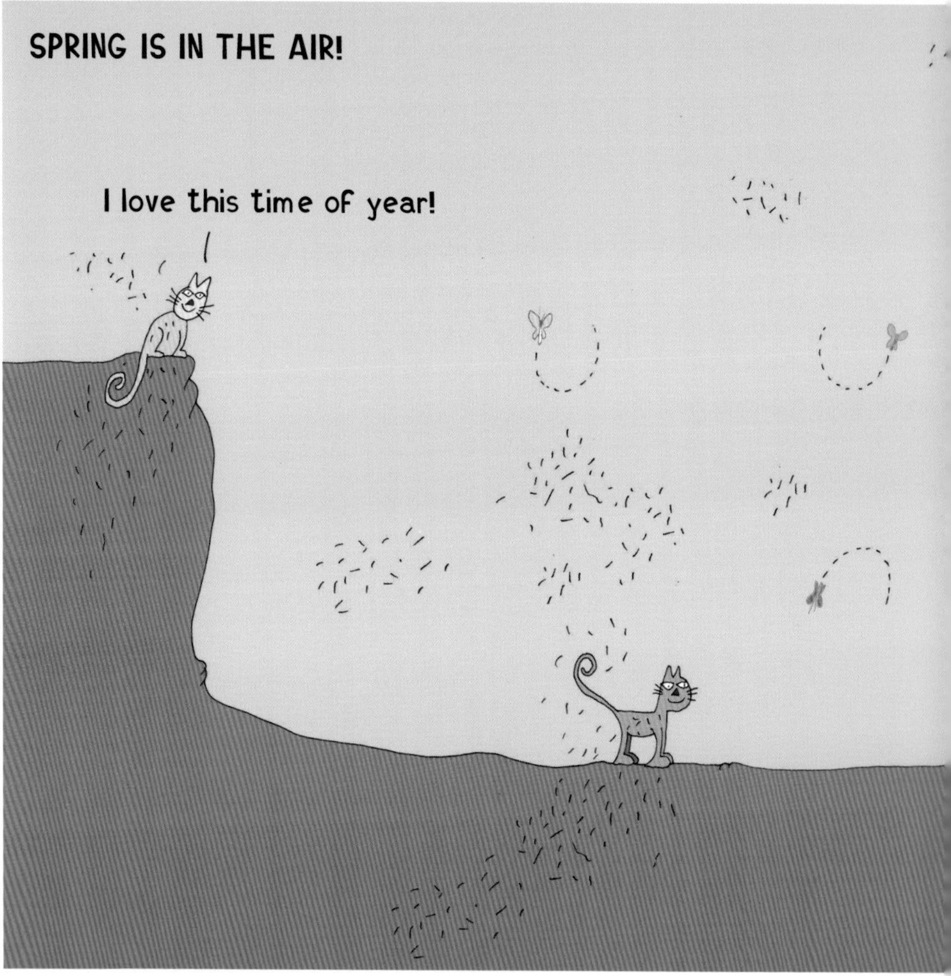
SPRING IS IN THE AIR!
I love this time of year!

CAT SURVIVAL GENE NUMBER 12: THE ABILITY TO COMPLETELY TURN OFF TO THE SOUND OF THE HUMAN VOICE.

ABOUT THE AUTHORS

Ralph Lazar and Lisa Swerling wrote this book on Robberg Beach, South Africa. Off-season they're based in the UK. Other series created by them include Harold's Planet and Epsilon Osborne, Hero of the Corporate Jungle.